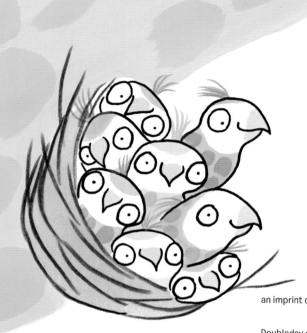

For travelers everywhere . . .
and for Tom—for being my home.

Published in the United States by Doubleday,
an imprint of Random House Children's Books, a division of Random House LLC,
a Penguin Random House Company, New York.

Doubleday and the colophon are registered trademarks of Random House LLC.

Visit us on the Web! randomhousekids.com

Educators and librarians, for a variety of teaching tools, visit us at RHTeachersLibrarians.com

Library of Congress Cataloging-in-Publication Data
Dicmas, Courtney, author, illustrator.
Home tweet home / by Courtney Dicmas. — First edition.
pages cm.
Summary: Cave swallows Burt and Pippi, tired of being crowded by their eight siblings,
set out to find a bigger nest but discover that traveling is good, but coming home is better.
ISBN 978-0-385-38535-0 (trade) — ISBN 978-0-375-97351-2 (lib. bdg.) — ISBN 978-0-385-38536-7 (ebook)
[1. Home—Fiction. 2. Brothers and sisters—Fiction. 3. Swallows—Fiction.] I. Title.
PZ7.D5623Hom 2015 [E]—dc23 2014012940

The illustrations for this book were created with gouache, acrylic,
and colored pencil on watercolor paper, and then digitally collaged.
Book design by Nicole de las Heras

MANUFACTURED IN CHINA

10 9 8 7 6 5 4 3 2 1

First Edition

HOME TWEET HOME

words & pictures by
Courtney Dicmas

Doubleday Books for Young Readers

High up on a cliff
above the shimmering sea,

there lived a family of cave swallows.

There were ten brothers and sisters:

Edgar, Maude, Rupert, Helena, Winnie, Cecil, Beatrix, Rosalie . . .

. . . Pippi and Burt.

Each night,
big brother Burt
looked at the moon
while big sister
Pippi worried.

"This nest is
too SMALL!"
Pippi grumbled.

"A bigger nest would have room for Rupert's stinky feet . . .

and Maude's judo . . .

and Cecil's band practice."

PHEEER ZWEE

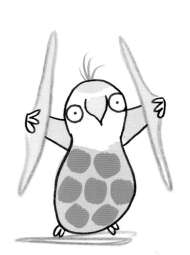

"Well, the world is BIG and so are we," chirped Burt.

"Let's go find somewhere BIG to live!"

So away they flew
into the night sky
to find a new place
to call home.

The next morning they found a spot that looked just right.

"This is PERFECT!" cheered Burt.

"It's BIG and sturdy! I wonder if we could live here."

Suurre yoouu caaan !

AAAAH!

"OH! That is VERY kind of you!" said Pippi.

"But I think perhaps we're looking for something a bit, uhm, softer. . . ."

The next time they were
more careful.

"This looks SO fluffy," sighed Pippi.

"I wonder if we could live . . ."

...and BOUNCY!

WHOOOOAAAA!

"Whew! That was close," squeaked Pippi.

"We were almost lunch."

"Now, this looks PERFECT," chirped Burt.

"Not too hard, not too soft, and not too pointy."

"I've always wanted to live on an island!" said Pippi.

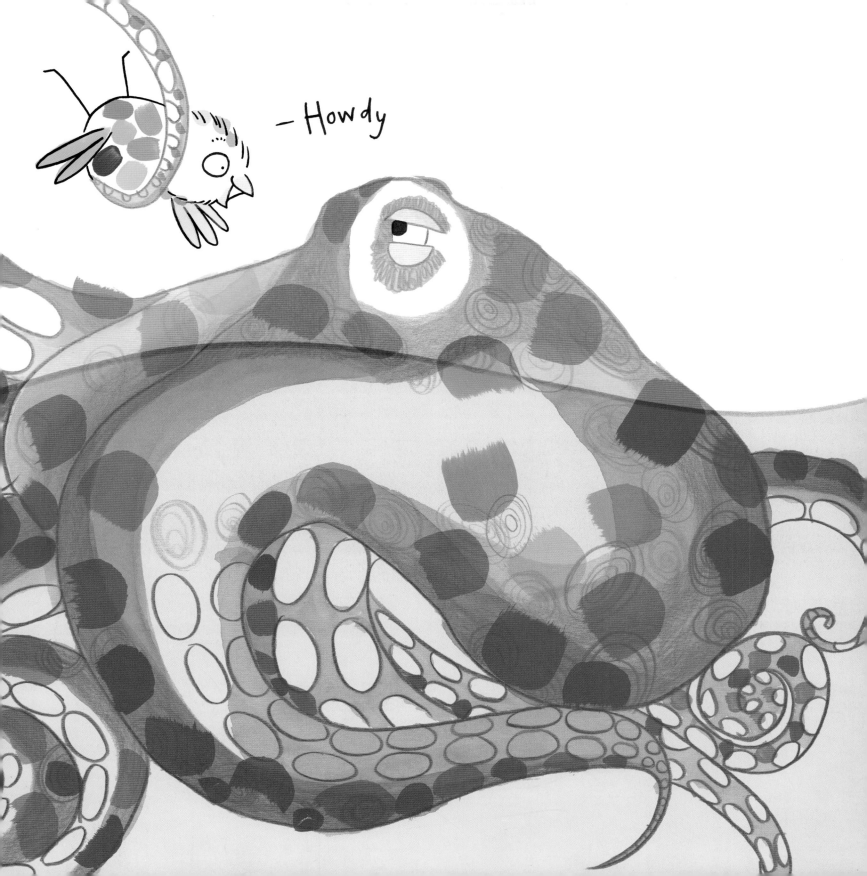

"This isn't what I thought it would be," sighed Burt.

"Can't we find someplace that's not so big . . .

or squishy . . .

or hungry?"

"That's

IT!!!"

"Burt, you're a GENIUS!"
cheered Pippi.

"I'm glad the world is so big,"
snoozed Burt. "It makes coming home
so much better."